HORRiD HENRY'S
School Fair

HORRiD HENRY'S
School Fair

Francesca Simon
Illustrated by Tony Ross

Orion
Children's Books

Horrid Henry's School Fair first appeared in *Horrid Henry's Haunted House*
First published in Great Britain in 1999 by Orion Children's Books
Reissued in paperback in 2008 by Orion Children's Books
This edition first published in Great Britain in 2018
by Hodder and Stoughton

1 3 5 7 9 10 8 6 4 2

Text copyright Francesca Simon, 1999
Illustrations copyright Tony Ross, 1999, 2018

A CIP catalogue record for this book
is available from the British Library.

ISBN 978 1 5101 0201 9

Printed and bound in China

The paper and board used in this book are made from wood
from responsible sources.

www.hachettechildrens.co.uk
www.horridhenry.co.uk

There are many more
Horrid Henry Early Reader books available.

For a complete list visit:
www.hachettechildrens.co.uk
or
www.horridhenry.co.uk

Contents

Chapter 1

"Henry! Peter! I need your donations to the school fair NOW!"

Mum was in a bad mood. She was helping Moody Margaret's mum organize the fair and had been nagging Henry for ages to give away some of his old games and toys.

Horrid Henry hated giving. He liked getting.

Horrid Henry stood in his bedroom.
Everything he owned was on the floor.

"How about giving away those bricks?" said Mum. "You never play with them any more."

"NO!" said Henry. They were bound to come in useful some day.

"How about some soft toys? When was the last time you played with Spotty Dog?"

"NO!" said Horrid Henry. "He's mine!"

Perfect Peter appeared in the doorway dragging two enormous sacks. "Here's my contribution to the school fair, Mum," said Perfect Peter.

Mum peeped inside the bags. "Are you sure you want to give away so many toys?" said Mum.

"Yes," said Peter. "I'd like other
children to have fun
playing with them."

"What a generous boy you are,
Peter," she said, giving him
a big hug.

Henry scowled. Peter could give away all his toys, for all Henry cared. Henry wanted to keep everything.

Chapter 2

Wait! How could he have forgotten?

Henry reached under his bed and
pulled out a large box hidden under
a blanket. The box contained all the
useless, horrible presents Henry had
ever received.

Packs of hankies.

Vests with ducks on them.

A nature guide.

Uggh! Henry hated nature. Why would anyone want to waste their time looking at pictures of flowers and trees?

And then, right at the bottom,
was the worst present of all.

A Walkie-Burpy-Slurpy-
Teasy-Weasy Doll.

He'd got it for Christmas from
a great-aunt he'd never met.
The card she'd written was
still attached.

Dear Henrietta
I thought this doll would be
perfect for a sweet little two-
year old like you!
Take good care of your new baby!
Love,
Great Aunt Greta.

Even worse, she'd sent Peter
something brilliant.

Dear Pete
You must be a teenager by now
and too old for toys, so here's
£25. Don't spend it all on sweets!
Love
Great Aunt Greta

Henry had screamed and begged, but Peter got to keep the money, and Henry was stuck with the doll. He was far too embarrassed to try to sell it, so the doll just lived hidden under his bed with all the other rotten gifts.

"Take that," said Henry, giving the doll a kick.

"Mama Mama Mama!" burbled the doll. "Baby burp!"

"Not Great-Aunt Greta's present!"
said Mum.

"Take it or leave it," said Henry.
"You can have the rest as well."

Mum sighed. "Some lucky children
are going to be very happy."
She took the hateful presents and put
them in the jumble sack.

Phew!
He'd got rid of that doll at last! He'd
lived in terror of Rude Ralph or
Moody Margaret coming over and
finding it. Now he'd never have to
see that burping slurping long-haired
thing again.

Chapter 3

Henry crept into the spare room where Mum was keeping all the donated toys and games for the fair. He thought he'd have a quick poke around and see what good stuff would be for sale tomorrow. That way he could make a dash and be first in the queue.

There were rolls of raffle tickets,
bottles of wine, the barrel for the
lucky dip, and sacks and sacks
of toys. Wow, what a hoard!
Henry just had to move that
rolled up poster out of the way
and start rummaging!

Henry pushed aside the poster
and then stopped. I wonder what
this is, he thought. I think I'll just
unroll it and have a little peek.
No harm in that.

Carefully, he untied the ribbon and laid the poster flat on the floor. Then he gasped.

This wasn't jumble. It was the Treasure Map! Whoever guessed where the treasure was hidden always won a fabulous prize.

Last year Sour Susan had won a skateboard.

The year before Jolly Josh had won a Super Soaker 2000.

Boy it sure was worth trying to find that treasure! Horrid Henry usually had at least five goes. But his luck was so bad he had never even come close.

Henry looked at the map.
There was the island, with its caves
and lagoons, and the sea surrounding
it, filled with whales and sharks
and pirate ships.

The map was divided into a hundred numbered squares. Somewhere under one of those squares was an X.

I'll just admire the lovely picture,
thought Henry.
He stared and stared.

No X.

He ran his hands over the map.
No X.

Henry sighed. It was so unfair! He never won anything. And this year the prize was sure to be a Super Soaker 5000.

Henry lifted the map to roll it up.
As he raised the thick paper to the
light, a large, unmistakable X was
suddenly visible beneath square 42.
The treasure was just under
the whale's eye.

He had discovered the secret.

"YES!" said Horrid Henry,
punching the air.
"It's my lucky day, at last!"

But wait. Mum was in charge of the
Treasure Map stall. If he was first
in the queue and instantly bagged
square 42 she was sure to
be suspicious.

So how could he let a few other children go first, but make sure none of them chose the right square?

And then suddenly, he had a
brilliant, spectacular idea . . .

Chapter 4

"Tra la la la la!" trilled Horrid Henry, as he, Peter, Mum and Dad walked to the school fair.

"You're cheerful today, Henry,"
said Dad.

"I'm feeling lucky," said
Horrid Henry.

He burst into the playground and
went straight to the Treasure
Map stall.

A large queue of eager children keen to pay 20p for a chance to guess had already formed. There was the mystery prize, a large, tempting, Super Soakersized box. Wheeee!

Rude Ralph was first in line.
"Psst, Ralph," whispered Henry.
"I know where X marks the spot.
I'll tell you if you give me 50p."

"Deal," said Ralph.
"92," whispered Henry.

"Thanks!" said Ralph. He wrote his name in square 92 and walked off, whistling.

Moody Margaret was next.

"Pssst, Margaret," whispered Henry.
"I know where X marks the spot."

"Where?" said Margaret.

"Pay me 50p and I'll tell you,"
whispered Henry.

"Why should I trust you?" said
Margaret loudly.

Henry shrugged. "Don't trust me
then, and I'll tell Susan," said Henry.

Margaret gave Henry 50p.

"2," whispered Horrid Henry.

Margaret wrote her name in square
2, and skipped off.

Henry told Lazy Linda the treasure
square was 4.

Henry told Dizzy Dave the treasure
square was 100.

Weepy William was told 22.

Anxious Andrew was told 14.

Then Henry thought it was time
he bagged the winning square. He
made sure none of the children he'd
tricked were nearby, then pushed
into the queue behind Beefy Bert.
His pockets bulged with cash.

"What number do you want, Bert?"
asked Henry's mum.

"I dunno," said Bert.

"Hi Mum," said Henry.
"Here's my 20p. Hmmm, now
where could that treasure be?"

Horrid Henry pretended to
study the map.
"I think I'll try 37," he said.
"No wait, 84. Wait, wait,
I'm still deciding . . ."

"Hurry up Henry," said Mum.
"Other children want to have a go."

"Okay, 42," said Henry.

Mum looked at him. Henry
smiled at her and wrote his
name in the square.

Then he sauntered off.

He could feel that Super Soaker in his hands already. Wouldn't it be fun to spray the teachers!

Chapter 5

Horrid Henry had a fabulous day.

He threw wet sponges at Miss Battle-Axe in the "Biff a Teacher" stall.

He joined in his class square dance.

He got a marble in the lucky dip.

Henry didn't even scream when
Perfect Peter won a box of notelets
in the raffle, and Henry didn't
win anything, despite spending
£3 on tickets.

"TIME TO FIND THE WINNER OF THE TREASURE MAP COMPETITION," boomed a voice over the playground.

Everyone stampeded to the stall.

Suddenly Henry had a terrible
thought. What if Mum had switched
the X to a different spot at the
last minute?

He couldn't bear it. He absolutely couldn't bear it. He had to have that Super Soaker!

Chapter 6

"And the winning number is . . ."

Mum lifted up the Treasure Map . . .

"42! The winner is – Henry."

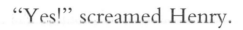

"Yes!" screamed Henry.

"What?" screamed Rude Ralph,
Moody Margaret, Lazy Linda,
Weepy William, and
Anxious Andrew.

"Here's your prize, Henry,"
said Mum.

She handed Henry the enormous
box. "Congratulations."
She did not look very pleased.

Eagerly, Henry tore off the paper.

His prize was a Walkie-Talkie-
Burpy-Slurpy-Teasy-
Weasy Doll.

"Mama Mama Mama!" burbled the
doll. "Baby Slurp!"

"AAARRGGGHHHH!"
howled Henry.

What are you going to read next?

Don't miss more mischief with
Horrid Henry . . .

Henry has a very
smelly plan to
defeat Margaret in
**Horrid Henry's
Stinkbomb,**

and battles with
Perfect Peter in
**Horrid Henry
and the Comfy
Black Chair**.

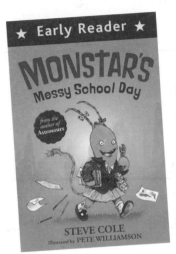

Or for more school stories, discover the magic of **Monstar's Messy School Day**,

and join the Weirdibeasts for fun and games in **Weird Sports Day**.

Visit
www.hachettechildrens.co.uk
or **www.horridhenry.co.uk**
to discover all the Early Readers